This is Truckdriver Tom. He
delivers parcels all around Story
Town in his trusty truck – and
sometimes he delivers people, too!

A catalogue record for this book is available from the British Library

Published by Ladybird Books Ltd
80 Strand London WC2R 0RL
A Penguin Company

4 6 8 10 9 7 5

Illustrations © Emma Dodd MMII

LADYBIRD and the device of a Ladybird are trademarks of Ladybird Books Ltd

Little Workmates

Truckdriver Tom

by Mandy Ross

illustrated by Emma Dodd

Early one morning,
Truckdriver Tom's
telephone rang.
It was Queen Clara.

"Please will you collect
a very special parcel
for me from the station?"
she asked.

"Certainly, Your Majesty,"
said Tom.

At Story Town Station, the stationmaster was waiting with the parcel.

It was enormous! Tom loaded it onto his truck and set off for the castle.

Brrrm, brrrm!

He hadn't gone far when he spotted PC Polly. She waved him to stop.

"My motorbike has broken down," called PC Polly. "Can you help me?"

"Of course" said Tom. And he wheeled the motorbike onto his truck.

"Climb in, PC Polly," he said. "I'll drop you at the Police Station."

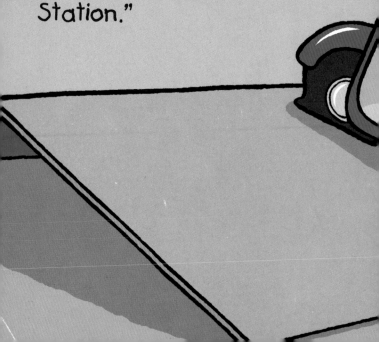

Brrrm, brrrm!

They hadn't gone far when they spotted Barker.

"But where's Mrs Dogsberry?" asked Tom.

Woof! Woof! Woof!

barked Barker.

Mrs Dogsberry had
tripped and hurt her knee.

"Climb in, Mrs Dogsberry,"
said Tom. "We'll drop you
at the hospital!"

Brrrm, brrrm!

Tom drove to Story Town hospital.

"Nurse Nancy will take care of you," he said. "I'll look after Barker until you get home."

"Thank you, Truckdriver Tom," said Mrs Dogsberry.

Brrrm, brrrm!

Next, Tom drove PC Polly to the Police Station.

"Hope your motorbike is fixed soon," he said.

"Thank you, Truckdriver Tom," said PC Polly.

Brrrm, brrrm!

Tom set off for home, when suddenly he remembered...

"Queen Clara's parcel!" He turned the truck around and drove straight to the castle, without stopping once.

Queen Clara opened the parcel straightaway. Inside was a brand new shiny bicycle.

Queen Clara couldn't wait to ride it.

Tom opened it straightaway. "A royal flag for my truck!" he gasped.

"It's to say thank you for being so helpful," smiled Queen Clara.

Truckdriver Tom was very happy as he drove home... and he didn't have to stop once!

This is Fireman Fergus. He is a brave firefighter and he has a good head for heights.

This is Nurse Nancy. She works hard looking after the patients at Story Town Hospital.

This is Builder Bill. He is a very good builder and his houses never fall down.

This is Queen Clara. She is a very good queen and all the people of Story Town love her.

This is Postman Pete. He loves delivering letters and parcels to everyone in Story Town.